BABAR

and that Rascal Arthur

LAURENT DE BRUNHOFF

Babar the King and Queen Celeste were
tired after a year of hard work and they set
out with their children for a holiday by the
sea. Here they are at Celesteville Station.

Pom, Flora, Alexander and Zephir the monkey climbed up to the overhead car. Babar's cousin, Arthur, wanted to go with them, but Babar said he was too big now.

7

During the journey, the three little elephants looked out of their windows and Arthur made faces at them from down below. It was great fun.

A little later, Zephir took Flora out in a boat and told her one of her favourite stories about a little mermaid.

At the end she said: "I should so like to see the little mermaid."

"But you can't," said Zephir. "She only appears if someone really needs her help."

Meanwhile, Pom and Alexander played at being little parcels which their father had to carry, one on his shoulder, the other tucked under his arm. They had to hold on tight while he hopped about.

Arthur had a plan of his own and slipped
away while Zephir and the other children
went shrimping. Flora found some crabs.

"Come and see my beautiful earrings!" she called to her brothers. But when Zephir took hold of one, it pinched him and hurt. His skin was not as tough as an elephant's.

But where was Arthur all this time?

He had found what he was after – the
great airfield nearby.

"This is more interesting than fishing!"
he thought.

14

Arthur had never seen so many
aeroplanes at one time before. The best one
of all was a green one. He longed to climb
up on its tail.

And what happened next? Elephants rushed onto the field to see the big green aeroplane take off . . . with Arthur on its tail.

He had just clambered up there when the plane began to move. He was terrified, but dared not jump. He clung on for dear life. First one, then another, of the elephants caught sight of him.

They all began to shout:
"He's going to fall! He's going to fall!"

Soon all they could see was a tiny spot of red on the aeroplane. "Come on," said the elephants. "We'd better go and inform the King at once. He'll be on the beach."

The pilot of the aeroplane threw out
a parachute, and Arthur managed to put
it on. Then he jumped. At first he fell like
a stone. Then the parachute opened. It
was fun – until a strong wind blew him
far, far from Baribarbotton.

19

He landed among some kangaroos.

"Well, big bird," said one, "where do you come from?"

"I'm not a bird," Arthur replied. "I can't fly. I was in a flying machine, a huge thing, very noisy. I came down by parachute."

Soon Arthur and the kangaroos were great friends.

Arthur got down on all fours to play with the babies. But he could not stay with them. He thought of Babar and Celeste waiting for him at home.

"Am I far from Baribarbotton?" he asked the kangaroos.

"Not very far," they told him. "We will show you the way."

The kangaroos took him to the station to catch a train home. They said over and over again, "You will come back, won't you, Mr Elephant?"

"Perhaps," Arthur replied. He was sorry to leave these nice new friends.

When the train came, it was not meant
for elephants, so Arthur had to travel in a
truck. Soon he fell fast asleep.

They came to a forest where little
monkeys often used to drop from the trees
to the roof of the trains for a ride. When
they saw Arthur, they cried: "Look what's
here! Let's play a trick on him!" And those
mischievous animals unhitched his truck.

23

"Oh dear, oh dear!" Arthur wailed when he woke up. "Now what has happened?"

He walked till he came to the bank of a river, where he met two dromedaries.

"Good day," he said. "My name is Arthur. I am the little cousin of Babar, King of the Elephants. Could you take me to Baribarbotton? I'm lost."

24

The dromedaries replied that they would
be delighted to take Arthur if he could think
of a way to cross the river, which was full of
crocodiles. Luckily a nice fat hippopotamus
and his brother offered to help.

25

And there, in no time, was a bridge of